Always Mom, Forever Dad

Joanna Rowland

Illustrated by Penny Weber

Tilbury House, Publishers
Thomaston, Maine

Tilbury House, Publishers
12 Starr Street
Thomaston, Maine 04861
800-482-1899
www.tilburyhouse.com

First hardcover edition: May, 2014 • 10 9 8 7 6 5 4 3 2 1
ISBN 978-0-88448-367-0
Text © 2014 by Joanna Rowland
Illustrations © 2014 by Penny Weber

Dedications:

For Katherine, Amber and Makenna.
Never doubt that you are loved. —JR

For my family —PW

Library of Congress Cataloging-in-Publication Data

Rowland, Joanna.
   Always Mom, forever Dad / by Joanna Rowland ; illustrated by Penny Weber. — First hardcover edition.
     pages cm

Summary: Children whose parents no longer live together discover that although much has changed, and
time spent with Mom is different than time spent with Dad, love is there no matter what.

 ISBN 978-0-88448-367-0 (hardcover : alk. paper)
 [1. Parent and child--Fiction. 2. Divorce--Fiction.] I. Weber, Penny, illustrator. II. Title.
  PZ7.R7972Alw 2014
  [E]--dc23
                         2013040077

Printed by Worzalla, Stevens Point, WI, USA.

When Mom and Dad moved apart, I was scared about what would change. They helped me see that even though things were different, one thing would never change. My mom and dad would always love me. And I know it's true.

When I'm with my dad, he makes me pancakes
for breakfast. He takes the whipped cream and
puts a happy face on them. I decorate his pancake
like a jellyfish and we laugh.

When I'm with my mom, she lets me
measure the ingredients to make banana
bread. When it's warm out of the oven,
she'll take out cookie cutters so we can
make the bread look like snowmen.

When I'm with my dad, sometimes we play in a small creek. All morning we jump from stone to stone looking for tadpoles to catch. If I'm lucky, a crawdad will walk by, ready for my pail.

At my mom's house, we have a bench swing on the deck. We like to look at the stars as we swing back and forth. I try to find animal faces in the starlit sky.

At my dad's house, when I'm sick, he makes me
chicken noodle soup. Then he reads me some
of our favorite books until I'm fast asleep.

At my mom's house, when I'm sick, we stay in our jammies all day. She finds a cozy blanket and watches my favorite movie with me.

When I'm with my dad and I accidentally knock over the block castle I've been building all day and want to cry, he helps me pick up the pieces. He says sometimes things fall apart so you can build something stronger than before.

When I'm with my mom and a
storm cancels our day at the zoo,
mom says changes can be hard,
but they can be exciting too.

She helps me imagine fun things to do on a rainy day.

When I'm with my dad, we catch snowflakes on our mittens, and I try to catch the biggest one. Then we make a snowman bigger than me.

When I'm with my mom, we set up a fort with blankets in the family room when it rains. We pretend we are camping, and she reads me my favorite stories by flashlight.

When I'm with my dad and I miss my mom, he sings me a song she used to sing to me when I was a baby. Then we call her to tell her all about our day.

When I'm with my mom and I miss my dad, she holds me on her lap while I draw things I like to do with my dad. After we put a stamp on the envelope, we call my dad to tell him he'll be getting a surprise in the mail.

At my dad's house when it's bedtime, he tells me stories about when he was a little boy before saying goodnight.

Then I kiss a picture of my mom and snuggle beneath the green blanket I've had since I was a baby.

At my mom's house when it's bedtime, I convince her to read me three stories. We say a special chant to the stars before a hug goodnight. Then I kiss a picture of my dad and go to sleep.

At my dad's house and at my mom's house, I am loved. And when I ask them how long they'll love me, they both reply always and forever. And I know it's true.